WELCOME TO CHINA

THE FLYING BUTTRESS CLASSICS LIBRARY is an imprint of:

NANTIER · BEALL · MINOUSTCHINE
Publishing co.
new york

TERRY AND HIS FRIEND PAT RYAN HAVE HIRED A BOAT BELONGING TO DALE SCOTT AND HER FATHER, OL' POP, IN WHICH THEY ARE GOING TO SEARCH FOR A HIDDEN MINE LEFT TERRY BY HIS GRANDFATHER......

11-5

GEE, MISS SCOTT - I'D HATE TO HAVE ANY TROUBLE BREAK WITH YOU ALONG!

I WAS THINKING THE SAME THING ABOUT YOU, TERRY!

- AW - I CAN TAKE CARE OF MYSELF!

.. I DON'T DOUBT THAT - BUT CONNIE TOLD THAT BIG TRAMP, POPPY JOE, ABOUT THIS TRIP - AND I'VE A HUNCH HE'LL TRY TO CUT HIMSELF IN!

NOT FAR BEHIND, POPPY JOE AND HIS HENCHMEN FOLLOW THE TREASURE BOAT..

KEEP THEM IN SIGHT, BUT DON'T LET THEM KNOW WE ARE FOLLOWING!

LOOKY HERE, CHINA BOY, YOU AIN'T DONE A LICK O' WORK SINCE WE STARTED ON THIS TREASURE HUNT!

ME COOKEE PLENTY EGGS! - NOW REST!

.. YOU NO WORK SO MUCH TOO! - HOW 'BOUT PLAY SOME FAN TAN?

WELL, I DON'T KEER IF I DO! - I RECKON I KIN SHOW YOU A THING ER TWO!

GO AHEAD, CHINA BOY! - I AIN'T BIN' LIVIN' IN CHINA ALL THESE YEARS WITHOUT LEARNIN' HOW T' PLAY FAN TAN!

HALF SPEED AHEAD!- HEY, POP!! ... WHAT'S THE MATTER WITH HIM, ANYWAY?

11-6

HEY POP! - HALF SPEED AHEAD! - CUT DOWN THAT ENGINE BEFORE WE RUN AGROUND!

GEE, MISS SCOTT! - MAYBE SUMTHIN'S WRONG WITH OL' POP!

HE NEVER DESERTED HIS ENGINE BEFORE! - GO BELOW, TERRY, AND SEE WHAT THE TROUBLE IS!

YES'M!

HEY, POP! - GET TO YOUR ENGINE! - DALE WANTS HALF SPEED AHEAD!

MY ENGINE!

.. TAIN'T MY ENGINE NO MORE! - YOU'LL HAVE T' GIVE ORDERS T' CHINA BOY! - HE JIST WON TH' BLOOMIN' THING!

11-7

TERRY, GET OUT THAT MAP YOUR GRANDFATHER LEFT YOU! - WE MUST BE NEARING THE LOCATION OF HIS MINE!

RIGHT'O, PAT!

ACCORDING TO THIS, WE TURN INTO LUN CHOW CREEK AND HEAD UP-STREAM!

GRANDPA SAID THIS WAS WILD COUNTRY! - WE'D BETTER BE CAREFUL!

11-8

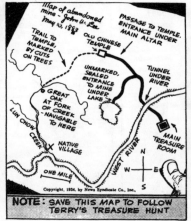

Map of abandoned mine - John U. Lee, May 12, 1863

PASSAGE TO TEMPLE. ENTRANCE UNDER MAIN ALTAR

TRAIL TO TEMPLE, MARKED BY CUTS ON TREES

OLD CHINESE TEMPLE

UNMARKED, SEALED ENTRANCE TO MINE UNDER LAKE

TUNNEL UNDER RIVER

GREAT OAK AT FORK OF CREEK - NAVIGABLE TO HERE

MAIN TREASURE ROOM

LUN CHOW CREEK

NATIVE VILLAGE

WEST RIVER

ONE MILE

N W S E

Copyright, 1934, by News Syndicate Co., Inc.

NOTE: SAVE THIS MAP TO FOLLOW TERRY'S TREASURE HUNT

AH, THEY TURN UP LUN CHOW CREEK! - COME! - WE GO, AS THE CROW FLIES, TO THE SHALLOW WATER WHERE THEY MUST ABANDON THEIR BOAT!

As Terry, Pat and Dale move on toward the abandoned mine they hear an explosion.... Fearing some harm may have befallen Ol' Pop, left behind to guard their boat, they send Connie back to investigate.....

11-19

GET GOIN', CHINA BOY! — REMEMBER, THREE SHOTS IF POP IS IN TROUBLE!

OH, SO MUCH WOE...

..AND ME NOT MAD AT ONE PERSON IN WORLD!

PEACE OF THE SOUL IS NOT FOR ME! WOULD THAT HONORABLE ANCESTORS HAD NOT INVENTED GUNPOWDER!

AH! — THE WITLESS ONE EMBARKS ON SOME MISSION — FOLLOW HIM!

GEE, PAT! — MAYBE WE SHOULDN'T HAVE SENT CONNIE BACK ALONE!

MAYBE IT'S A TRAP! — IF WE ARE TO BE ATTACKED WE'LL NEED FULL STRENGTH — AND WE CAN SPARE 'HIM BETTER THAN ANY OF US!

MILTON CANIFF Copyright, 1934, by News Syndicate Co., Inc.

HELP! — I'M AGITIN' WEAK! — THEY MUSTA HEARD TH' BLOWUP!

11-20

HELLO! — IT IS I!! — VELLY SURE SOME PERSON MAKE SOUND LIKE MOAN OF PAIN!

MILTON CANIFF

OH, MERCY INDEED!

ALL IS SAVED! — COMES CONNIE! — FIRST CLASS RESCUE CLOPPITY CLOP! HOLD THE FORTRESS!!

DROP THE WEAPON, STUPID ONE! MAKE A MOVE, AND YOU ARE DEAD CHINESE!

AND I FORGET TO SHOOT THREE TIMES!

MORE WOE!

Copyright, 1934, by News Syndicate Co., Inc.

TALK!! — WHERE DO THE AMERICANS GO TO FIND TREASURE?

NO TELL! — ONE TIME PREVIOUS CONNIE MAKE TOO MUCH SPEECH!

11-21

TELL ME, YOU INFERIOR WORM, OR I SHALL HANG YOU BY YOUR BIG EARS!!

OH, NO! — I TELL! THEY GO BY OLD TEMPLE! — COME, I SHOW!

YOU HEATHEN TRAITOR!

FORGIVE, PLEASE! — HANG BY EARS HURT MOST PLENTY!

DRESS THE ANCIENT ONE'S BURNS! — WE WILL USE THEM BOTH AS HOSTAGES!

FUNNY WE DON'T HEAR FROM CONNIE!

HE DIDN'T SHOOT — SO EVERYTHING MUST BE OKAY!

MILTON CANIFF

STILL NO DANGER SIGNAL FROM CONNIE — GUESS WE WERE UNDULY ALARMED!

LOOK! — HERE'S — ANOTHER MARK! — WE MUST BE NEAR THE OLD TEMPLE!

11-22

YEAH — AND THE MINE DOOR IS HIDDEN UNDER THE MAIN ALTAR!

GEE, DALE! — IF THIS MINE IS AS RICH AS GRANDPA SAID — WE'LL BE ROLLIN' IN DOUGH!

WELL, TERRY — THAT MUST BE THE PLACE!

GOLLY! — IT'S SPOOKY!

IT GIVES ME THE CREEPS, TOO! — SOMETHING SINISTER ABOUT IT!

MILTON CANIFF

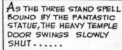

TERRY, PAT AND DALE, HIDDEN BEHIND THE ALTAR GOD IN THE OLD CHINESE TEMPLE WATCH POPPY JOE AND HIS MEN AS THEY SEARCH FOR WHAT THEY THOUGHT WOULD BE THE DEAD BODIES OF THE AMERICANS...

THE FOREIGN DEVILS COULD NOT HAVE VANISHED INTO THIN AIR!

THEY'RE BOUND TO FIND US! — WHEN THEY DO — LET 'EM HAVE IT!

12-3

AT THIS MOMENT THE STRANGE CREATURE, WHO HAS WATCHED THE SCENE FROM THE EYE OF THE GREAT STATUE, PLACES A BLOW GUN TO HIS LIPS — THERE IS A SOFT THUD — AND ONE OF THE BANDITS FALLS WITH A DART IN HIS THROAT!

OW!

Copyright, 1934, by News Syndicate Co., Inc.

MILTON CANIFF

FER PETE'S SAKE! — ONE O' TH' CHINKS HAS BEEN HIT BY AN ARROW — OR SUMTHIN'!

12-4

ANOTHER SOFT THUD — AND A SECOND BANDIT FALLS WITH A DART IN HIS NECK

THE AMERICANS! — BEHIND THE IDOL! — GET THE DOGS!

QUICK, PAT! — THEY'VE SEEN US! — THEY THINK WE SHOT THE ARROWS!

STAY UNDER COVER, DALE! — OKAY, TERRY! — GIVE 'EM THE WORKS!

Copyright, 1934, by News Syndicate Co., Inc.

MILTON CANIFF

DISCOVERED BY POPPY JOE, TERRY AND PAT EMPTY THEIR GUNS AT THE BANDITS — THEN FIGHT IT OUT — HAND TO HAND!!

12-5

Copyright, 1934, by News Syndicate Co., Inc.

SO! YAH GOTTA KNIFE, EH? — WELL, I CAN PLAY ROUGH, TOO!

COME! — I CUT OUT THE MELICAN TONGUE!

NOT WHILE I STILL REMEMBER HOW TO TAKE OUT THE SAFETY MAN!

MILTON CANIFF

COME ON, YOU RICE BURNER! — I CAN LICK YOU IN SPITE OF YOU BEIN' TWICE MY SIZE! — I'M JIST STARTIN'!

12-6

LIKE A PANTHER THE BANDIT SPRINGS! — TERRY IS CAUGHT OFF BALANCE...

Copyright, 1934, by News Syndicate Co., Inc.

BUT, AS THE GLEAMING KNIFE COMES DOWN — THE FACE APPEARS AGAIN IN THE EYE OF THE STATUE! — A DART SPEEDS ON ITS WAY..

AND THE ORIENTAL SINKS SLOWLY TO THE FLOOR......

MILTON CANIFF

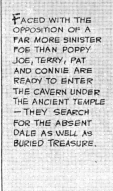

FACED WITH THE OPPOSITION OF A FAR MORE SINISTER FOE THAN POPPY JOE, TERRY, PAT AND CONNIE ARE READY TO ENTER THE CAVERN UNDER THE ANCIENT TEMPLE — THEY SEARCH FOR THE ABSENT DALE AS WELL AS BURIED TREASURE.

12-17

YOUR GRANDFATHER'S MAP SHOWS ONLY ONE OTHER ENTRANCE TO THIS MINE—WHOEVER CARRIED DALE AWAY MUST BE SOMEWHERE IN THE PASSAGE!

LET'S GET GOIN'!—SHE'LL NEED US!

THIS IS NO ABANDONED MINE! —SOMEONE'S BEEN USING THE PLACE PLENTY!

OOOH! SUCH GREAT AREAS OF NO-LIGHT! —A FIT HOME FOR NONE BUT BATS!

I DON'T SEE A THING!—BUT I GOT A FEELIN' WE'RE BEIN' WATCHED!

MILTON CANIFF

© by Chicago Tribune-N.Y. News Syndicate, Inc.

THEY MUSTA DRAGGED POOR DALE DOWN THROUGH HERE!

CONNIE ALL OVER BUMPS OF THE DUCK!

THERE ARE FRESH MARKS IN THE DUST! —I THINK WE'RE GETTING WARM!

12-18

SUDDENLY, JUST AHEAD, A HEAVY DOOR DROPS AND COMPLETELY BLOCKS THE PASSAGE

OOH!

HEY!

WHAT TH' DICKENS!

THEN, JUST BEHIND, ANOTHER DOOR SLIDES DOWN! THEY ARE PRISONERS !!!

A TRAP!

MY GOSH! —WE'RE BOXED IN!

DISASTER APLENTY—AND THEN SOME!

MILTON CANIFF © by Chicago Tribune-N.Y. News Syndicate, Inc.

THIS IS TOUGH! —HOW CAN WE FIGHT SOMEONE WE CAN'T EVEN SEE?

PAT! LOOK! —BEHIND YOU!

12-19 © by Chicago Tribune-N.Y. News Syndicate, Inc.

I WILL BE BRIEF, FOOLHARDY ONES! —YOU ARE HELPLESS! —SURRENDER YOUR WEAPONS AT ONCE, OR SUFFER MY WRATH!

GOLLY! WHAT A FACE!

THE FAIR WHITE LADY ALREADY GRACES MY MASTER'S DUNGEON! —DECIDE QUICKLY!

SO IT'S LIKE THAT? —YOU TURN THE GIRL OVER TO US—OR I'LL CLIMB UP THERE AND BREAK YOUR DIRTY NECK!

TELL 'IM, PAT!

THE LION IN THE CAGE IS BUT A PATHETIC SHADOW OF THE KING OF THE JUNGLE! —LITTLE CARE I FOR YOUR TINY LIVES! —I LEAVE YOU TO YOUR FATE!

MILTON CANIFF

I GIVE YOU ONE MORE CHANCE! —HAND OVER YOUR WEAPONS AND SURRENDER!—OR YOU DIE!

WHO DOES HE THINK HE IS?!

HERE'S YOUR ANSWER!

THE TRAP DOOR SLAMS SHUT AS PAT OPENS FIRE.. © by Chicago Tribune-N.Y. News Syndicate, Inc.

THE TRAMP KNOWS HE HAS US IN A SPOT!

12-20

WHAT'S THAT?

I HEAR IT! —IT'S A HISSING NOISE!—SOUNDS LIKE RUNNING WATER!

MILTON CANIFF

IT IS WATER! THEY'RE FLOODING THE TUNNEL !!!

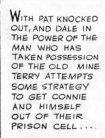

WITH PAT KNOCKED OUT, AND DALE IN THE POWER OF THE MAN WHO HAS TAKEN POSSESSION OF THE OLD MINE, TERRY ATTEMPTS SOME STRATEGY TO GET CONNIE AND HIMSELF OUT OF THEIR PRISON CELL....

12-31

HELP! THIS GUY'S GONE BATTY!

GET HOT, CONNIE! —TH' GUARD'S COMIN' ON TH' RUN!

YOWEE! WHOOPDEDOODLE! GETTIN' MORE NUTSIER BY EACH MINUTE!!!

WHAT MAKES SUCH MUCH BIG SOUND?

QUICK, MISTER! —IT'S THIS CHINK! —HE'S CRAZY! —I'M AFRAID HE'LL KILL ME —ER SUMTHIN'!!

NO CAN KILL YOU! —MASTER SAVE YOU FOR BIG TORTURE BYMBY!

I KNOW!—AN' I WOULDN'T DISAPPOINT YOUR MASTER FOR ANYTHING! —OH, SAVE ME DEAR SIR! —YOU ARE SO STRONG!

Copyright, 1934, by Chicago Tribune-N. Y. News Syndicate Inc.

GRAB HIM, MISTER! —HE'S A DANGEROUS LOONEYTICK! —HE SAID HE'D KILL ME!

COME WITLESS ONE! I SHAVE OFF YOUR OVERSIZE EARS!

HI-DIDDLE-DOODLE! —WATCH DUT FOR PROPELLER! —CONNIE GONNA TAKE OFF! —PUTT! PUTT! WHRRRR!

1-1   Copyright, 1935, by Chicago Tribune-N. Y. News Syndicate Inc.

OKAY, CONNIE! —HEAVE!

TOOT! TOOT! POOSH 'EM UP! —OVER FENCE IS OUT! — COMES STRAIGHT ARM! CONNIE ALL CHINA SWAY BACK LAST SEASON!!

OOMP!

WHO GOT OVERTIME EARS, NOW? —HOTSY DANDY! —HOW YOU LIKE, SPORT?

MILTON CANIFF

RIDEUM, COW GENTLEMAN! CONNIE NUMBER ONE COW POKER OF CHINA! —BEEN THROWUM BULL LONG TIME!

WHAT ARE THEY DOIN' WITH TH' AMERICAN LADY? —TALK OR I'LL POKE YER PEEPERS!

UCK!

1-2   Copyright, 1935, by Chicago Tribune-N. Y. News Syndicate Inc.

—UCK! —MASTER HAVE MUCH CEREMONY IN THRONE ROOM! —AWK! —MAKE WHITE FLOWER SLAVE GIRL! —MAYBE SO MAKE MARRY ALSO! GLUP! GLOWP!

CHILLYO, VL'INEGAR FACE! —IP RATS BITE, JUS' TALK TO 'EM LIKE BROTHER! — NO TROUBLE FOR YOU! TOODLE YOODLE!

LOCK 'IM IN, CONNIE! —WE GOTTA SAVE DALE FROM OL' PRETZEL CHEST!

GOSH! —HERE THEY COME! —THEY'VE GOT DALE ALL FIXED UP IN CHINESE CLOTHES TO MEET TH' BIG CHEESE!

LET'S BUSTUM UP PARTY! —CONNIE PLENTY TOUGH TODAY! —ALMOST SCARED OF SELF!!

MILTON CANIFF

OOOH! GUARD KINDA BIG! —MAYBE CONNIE NO SO TOUGH AS CONNIE THOUGHT!

GO BOW BEFORE MASTER!

SSHHH! —THEY'LL HEAR US!

1-3   MILTON CANIFF

THERE'S A BALCONY AROUND THAT THRONE ROOM —COME ON —LET'S GO UP THERE!

ALLITE! —CONNIE DO ANYTHING TO KEEP MISSY DALE FROM MARRY OL' PHUTZ FACE!

GEE! —HE'S GOT HIS GANG WITH HIM! —IF WE COULD JUS' DO SOMETHIN' TO CATCH 'EM ALL OFF THEIR GUARD AT ONCE!

AH! —MY LOVELY WHITE FLOWER HAS WISELY CHOSEN NOT TO RESIST THE CHARMS OF THIS ALL POWERFUL PERSON! —COME, LITTLE BLOSSOM! —YOU MAY KISS OUR HAND!

Copyright, 1935, by Chicago Tribune-N. Y. News Syndicate Inc.

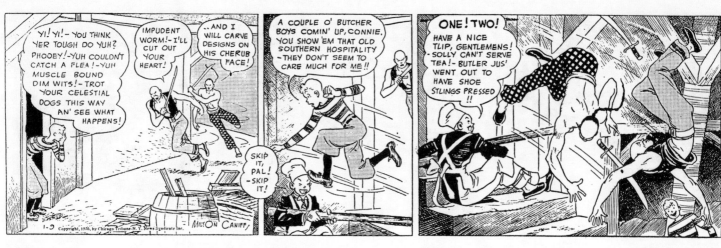

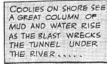

WHILE TERRY, PAT AND CONNIE ARE LAMENTING BEING BROKE IN A STRANGE COUNTRY, TERRY SEES A THIEF GRAB A LADY'S PURSE—HE TACKLES THE THUG

EAT DIRT, YOU BLOKE!—AN' YOU OUGHTA BE GLAD I'M NOT FEELIN' MEAN TODAY!

OW! GLUB!

NOW SCRAM!—I'D TURN YAH OVER TO TH' COPS, BUT I FEEL BIG HEARTED—AN' TH' LADY GETS HER PURSE BACK ANYHOW!

HOW SURPRISING!—THE URCHIN DID NOT TRY TO ABSCOND WITH THE PURSE HIMSELF! AMAZING—YES, QUITE!

HERE Y'ARE, MISS!

OH—THANK YOU SO MUCH!

I SUPPOSE ONE IS EXPECTED TO REWARD THE MOPPET!—HERE—NOW RUN ALONG, AND DO NOT ANNOY THE LADY!—COME NOW!—ON YOUR WAY, SMALL BOY!

WHY YOU..!

TH' BIG LUG!—HE CALLED ME AN URCHIN!—AN'A MOPPET!—AN'A SMALL BOY!—AN' HE HANDS ME MONEY AS IF I WUZ A PANHANDLER!—I SHOULDA PUT A DENT IN HIS BIG BEAK!—WOW!—AM I BURNED UP!

NOW THAT YOU'VE DONE YOUR GOOD DEED, COME ALONG!—I JUST REMEMBERED A MAN I KNOW IN THIS TOWN—BOY, ARE YOU THE BIG HERO!

BUT TH' GUY INSULTED ME!

DMITRI, YOU WERE RATHER UNKIND TO THAT BOY WHO RECOVERED MY PURSE!—I THOUGHT HE WAS VERY NICE ABOUT IT!

COME, COME, MY DEAR!—HE PROBABLY RECOGNIZED YOU AND HOPED TO PUT YOU IN HIS DEBT!—BUT I DISMISSED HIM DIDN'T I?—AH INDEED YES!—QUITE!

MY FRIEND LIVES AT THIS CLUB!—LET'S HOPE HE'S IN!

HOT DOG!—ONE OF THOSE SNOOTY EUROPEAN CLUBS!—THIS GUY MUST BE A BIG SHOT!

COME, COME, YOU BLIGHTAHS—WE'LL 'AVE NO BLOOMIN' LOITERIN' 'ERE!

I WANT TO SEE DOCTOR McANDREWS THE EXPLORER!—TELL HIM IT'S PAT RYAN CALLING!

NONSENSE!—THE DOCTOR 'AS NO TIME FOR THE LIKES O' YOU!—MOVE ON!—WE WANT NO TRAMPS 'ANGING ABOUT THIS 'YERE ENTRANCE!!

DOC!—YOU'RE JUST IN TIME!—THE DUKE OF THE CANOPY JUST GAVE US THE BUM'S RUSH!

HELLO PAT! BY JOVE I'M GLAD TO SEE YOU!—BRING YOUR FRIENDS INSIDE WHERE WE CAN TALK!

TRAMP! TRAMP! TRAMP! THE BOYS ARE MARCHING!

WELL, PAT—WHAT'S ON YOUR MIND?—YOU AND YOUR FRIENDS LOOK AS THOUGH YOU'VE HAD SOME BAD BREAKS!

FRANKLY, DOC—WE'RE BROKE!—WE NEED A STAKE—AND A PLACE TO BUNK FOR AWHILE!

THAT'S EASILY FIXED! HERE, BOY!—SHOW THESE MEN TO MY QUARTERS! THEY CAN FRESHEN UP THERE—MAKE THEM COMFORTABLE!

VELLY GOOD, SIRE!

HONORABLE DOCTOR SAY ME TAKE YOUR MASTERS' LUGGAGE UP TO ROOM—! WHERE IS SAME?

HMMM!—VELLY AWKWARD! MASTERS HAVE NO LUGGAGE—BUT CONNIE MUST IMPRESS BOY SO TO BE BIG SHOT!

?

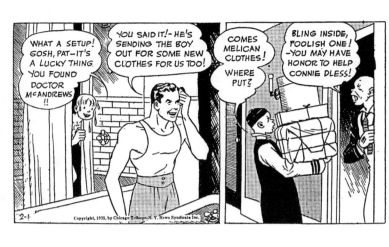

Dear Boys—

Pay no attention to anything I had to say to you before my niece — I have never been more pleased than when I heard Pat had hit Dmitri! — I've often wanted to do it myself.

I have reason to believe the dear Count may be an imposter! — Will you check with Hong Kong police?—

C. Drake

WO-O-U

NO USE TRYING TO HOLD OFF NATIVES! GET THE LAUNCH READY. WE'LL CLEAR OUT OF HERE TONIGHT!

RIGHT'O WEAZEL

GET THAT THING GOIN'!

BLIGH'ME, WEAZEL! TH' BLOOMIN' ENGINE WON'T START!

SUDDENLY THE WEIRD SOUND CEASES AND THEN BEGINS A STEADY DISTANT RUMBLE.

DISASTER! DISASTER!

WAR DRUMS!

I'VE HEARD THEY ALWAYS DO THAT JUST BEFORE AN ATTACK!

KEEP IT UP CONNIE! IT'S BEGINNING TO GET 'EM!

BOOM TIDDY! BOOM TIDDY! HOT DOG! ALWAYS WANTED TO BE DLUMMER BOY!!

BOOM BOOM

OIL

BOOM! BOOM! BOOM! BOOM!

COME ON, YOU COWARDS! THEY CAN'T BE AS WELL ARMED AS WE! HOLD A GUN ON THE GIRL, COOK! - NO NATIVES CAN SCARE ME!

As SOON AS WEAZEL AND HIS MEN START TOWARD CONNIE'S HIDING PLACE, DRAKE, ACROSS THE ISLAND, STARTS A MONOTONOUS BEATING ON ANOTHER EMPTY OIL CAN....

LISTEN - MORE DRUMS OVER THERE!

BOOM! BOOM! BOOM! BOOM!

BLAST YE WEAZEL - I AIN'T FIGHTIN' NO SAVAGES I CAN'T EVEN SEE!

Reg. U.S. Pat. Off.: Copyright, 1935, by Chicago Tribune-N. Y. News Syndicate, Inc.

ALL RIGHT, YOU YELLOW RATS -! - I CAN'T GO IT ALONE - FALL BACK AND WE'LL MAKE A STAND AT THE BOAT!

THEIR BOAT'S OUT OF COMMISSION! WHAT NOW PAT?

GOOD! KEEP UP THE INSOMNIA SERENADE AWHILE LONGER, CONNIE! - THEN WE'LL LEAVE THEM TO DREAM THEY'RE PLAYING A LEADING ROLE IN A CANNIBAL STEW!

I - LOVE A PARADE

BOOM BO B

MILTON CANIFF

3-30

UNABLE TO COME OUT IN THE OPEN AND FIGHT WITH WEAZEL'S WELL ARMED GANG, TERRY AND PAT TRY WEARING THEM DOWN BY IMITATING NATIVE DRUMS IN THE JUNGLE

NORMANDIE ADDS TO THE HORROR BY SCREAMING ALL THROUGH THE NIGHT...

4-1

THOSE INFERNAL DRUMS HAVE STOPPED! BUT IT'S NEARLY DAWN - THAT BLAZING SUN WILL SOON BE BEATING DOWN!

IT'S DRIVING ME CRAZY!

SHUT UP! YOU'RE NO WORSE OFF THAN US!

GOT TO HAND IT TO THE DRAKE GIRL! SHE'S PUTTING ON A GREAT ACT! - GET THE LAST LITTLE GADGET READY, CONNIE! ...

ALL HOTSY, FIXUP, MIST'PAT! THIS MAKE BAD FELLERS GET BUMPS OF DUCK ALL OVER!

LET'S GO TO TH' BEACH!

Reg. U.S. Pat. Off.: Copyright, 1935, by Chicago Tribune-N. Y. News Syndicate, Inc.

STEADY CONNIE!

WHOOPSY DOOPSY! LIKE OPENING ACT IN VLAUDY VILLE SHOW!

SHH! THEY'LL HEAR US!

MILTON CANIFF

IT'S LIGHT ENOUGH TO SEE, NOW! LIMEY YOU GO UP THE BEACH! COUNT, YOU GO DOWN! FIND THOSE NATIVES' TRACKS SO WE'LL KNOW HOW MANY WE'RE FACING!

RIGHT'O

4-2 Reg. U.S. Pat. Off.: Copyright, 1935, by Chicago Tribune-N. Y. News Syndicate, Inc.

THE GROUND IS SO HARD ON THIS HILL WHERE THE DRUMS WERE BEATING THAT THEY DIDN'T LEAVE A MARK! -

BLIGH'ME, I DON'T LIKE THIS BUSINESS A BIT! - ENOUGH TO DRIVE A BLOKE BATTY!

MILTON CANIFF

SUDDENLY THERE IS A YELL FROM UP THE BEACH... WEAZEL RUSHES TO THE SPOT WHERE LIMEY STANDS SHAKING IN HIS BOOTS...

WHAT IS IT, LIMEY? WHAT'S EATIN' YOU?

NUTHIN'-YET! - OOOH! LOOK AT THEM TRACKS! TH' BEAST THAT LEFT 'EM MUST WEIGH 400 POUNDS, EASY!

LIMEY AND THE COUNT HAVE OPENLY REBELLED AGAINST WEAZEL'S LEADERSHIP — AND NORMANDIE LOSES NO TIME TELLING WEAZEL THAT HIS TWO CONFEDERATES ARE PLOTTING TO TURN ON HIM....

4-17

TH' DIRTY RATS! SO THEY THINK THEY CAN BUMP ME OFF AND COLLECT ALL THE RANSOM DOUGH THEMSELVES!

WAIT! DON'T DO ANYTHING FOOLISH, MR. WEAZEL!

THEY'RE TWO AGAINST ONE! — IF ANYTHING HAPPENS TO YOU I DON'T KNOW **WHAT** I'LL DO!

YEAH! I'D BETTER COOK UP SOME EXCUSE TO GET THEIR GUNS FIRST! — THANKS!

LATER IN THE DAY WHILE WEAZEL IS TAKING HIS TURN ON WATCH IN THE BLAZING HEAT — NORMANDIE MANAGES TO GET THE OTHER TWO ALONE...

Reg. U.S. Pat. Off.:
Copyright, 1935, by Chicago
Tribune-N. Y. News Syndicate, Inc.

SHHH! — SPEAK IN WHISPERS! WEAZEL IS PLOTTING TO GET YOUR GUNS SO HE CAN TAKE ME HOME AND COLLECT ALL THE RANSOM MONEY — I THINK HE TAMPERED WITH THE BOAT MOTOR DELIBERATELY! — I'M SO AFRAID!

WOT?

GIVE ME YOUR GUNS — WE'LL KEEP 'EM IN A CENTRAL STACK SO WE CAN GET AT 'EM EASY IN CASE OF AN ATTACK!

SO THAT'S YER GAME!

4-18

NO, NO! — DON'T DO IT, LIMEY! — HE WANTS TO KILL US! — WE KNOW TOO MUCH!

TAKE IT EASY, COUNT! — NOW LOOKIT 'ERE, WEAZEL — YOU KNOW THAT AIN'T SENSIBLE!

I KNOW WHAT YOU TWO RATS ARE UP TO — IF YOU THINK YOU CAN RUB ME OUT AND COLLECT THE RANSOM DOUGH YERSELVES, — YER CRAZY!

'EY, WAIT!

FERGIT THAT RANSOM TALK! WE GOTTA WORRY ABOUT SAVIN' OUR 'IDES FROM THEM BLOODY CANNIBALS!

DON'T TRY TO SOFT SOAP ME!

FIGHT, YOU DOGS! — I DON'T THINK IT WILL BE VERY LONG NOW!

Reg. U.S. Pat. Off.:
Copyright, 1935, by Chicago
Tribune-N. Y. News Syndicate, Inc.

I DON'T CARE WHAT YE THINK O' ME, WEAZEL! — I ONLY GOT ONE IDEA RIGHT NOW — AN' THAT'S TO GIT OFF THIS ISLAND ALIVE! — AN' I ADVISE YE TO DO TH' SAME!

4-19

As LIMEY TRIES TO CALM WEAZEL'S TEMPER, THE COUNT WANDERS TOWARD THE SPRING — HE IS SO THIRSTY AND CRAZED BY THE HEAT THAT HE MUST HAVE WATER AT ANY COST...

Reg. U.S. Pat. Off.
Copyright, 1935, by Chicago
Tribune-N. Y. News Syndicate, Inc.

POISON! WHAT DO I CARE... GOING TO DIE ANYHOW... GOT TO HAVE WATER!

ABOUT THIS SAME TIME, TERRY STARTS DOWN TO THE OUTLAWS' SPRING TO REPLENISH THE PEA SOUP THAT MAKES THE WATER LOOK POISONED...

FINISH SHAVIN' PAT — I'LL FIX TH' SPRING! THEY WON'T SEE ME!

WATER! WATER! I'M GOING TO DRINK — POISON OR NO POISON!

As TERRY ARRIVES AT THE OUTLAWS' SPRING TO REPLENISH THE "POISON", HE SEES THE COUNT ABOUT TO TAKE A DRINK...

4-20

WATER! WATER! I DON'T CARE IF IT **IS** POISON! BETTER TO DIE THAN BE TORTURED!

OH MY GOSH! HE'S TAKIN' A DRINK! NOW HE'LL KNOW THE SPRING AIN'T REALLY POISONED! — FER PETE'S SAKE!

OW!

IT'S WORKIN' ALREADY! I'M DYIN'!!!

Between the howls of the Mad Count and the rumble of what they think are native drums, plus their burning thirst, Normandie's captors are nearly at the breaking point... – Just at dawn they see the water bottle on the beach...

4-26

Reg. U.S. Pat. Off.:
Copyright, 1938, by Chicago
Tribune-N. Y. News Syndicate, Inc.

LOOK WEAZEL! A WATER BOTTLE FROM TH' YACHT!

WATER BOTTLE?

HOLD ON! I SEEN IT FIRST!

IT'S STILL CORKED – AN' THERE'S WATER IN IT – FRESH WATER!

'EY WHAT'S THIS? – YOU MEAN T' HOG IT?

THERE AIN'T MUCH HERE – AN' ALL OF IT'S MINE!

I STUCK UP FER YE ONCE! – NOW, YE WON'T EVEN GIVE A PAL A DRINK O' WATER, YE BILGE RAT!

IT'S MINE, I TELL YAH! MINE!

4-27

– AN' I'LL FIX YOU SO YOU WON'T EVER GET ANY OF IT!

OW!

BAM!

WEAZEL SWIFTLY UNCORKS THE BOTTLE AND TAKES A DEEP GULP....

Reg. U. S. Pat. Off.:
Copyright, 1938, by Chicago
Tribune-N. Y. News Syndicate, Inc.

KEROSENE!!

After shooting Limey over possession of a water bottle he thinks has drifted up from the wrecked yacht, Weazel takes a deep swallow of the contents before he realizes it is KEROSENE!

4-29

AWK! KEROSENE!! I'M BURNIN' UP INSIDE! – OW!

WEAZEL STUMBLES BACK TO THE BEACH, DESPERATELY ILL FROM THIRST, AND THE EFFECTS OF THE KEROSENE...

HE'S THE LAST ONE! – THIS WILL BE THE SHOW DOWN! I FEEL IT COMING!!

WEAZEL'S DROOPIN' LIKE A WEEPIN' WILLOW! LET'S RUSH HIM AN' GET IT OVER!

WHOA, PAL! HE'S STILL ARMED TO THE TEETH – AND OUT ON THAT OPEN BEACH! – HE'D SEE US COMING AND KILL NORMANDIE BEFORE WE COULD GET HIM! – LET THE SUN WORK ON HIM FIRST!

Reg. U. S. Pat. Off.:
Copyright, 1938, by Chicago Tribune-N. Y. News Syndicate, Inc.

I CAN'T STAND THIS SUSPENSE! LET'S GET THAT GUY BEFORE HE TAKES A SHOT AT MISS DRAKE!

DON'T GET SO HOPPED UP! HE'S STILL DYNAMITE! – LOOK! SHE'S GOING AFTER HIS GUN! – OH, THAT'S A MISTAKE!

4-30

WOT TH'! – SO YOU WAS GONNA NICK ME FOR MY GUN! YAH LITTLE TRAMP!

GIT AWAY FROM ME! ALL MY BAD LUCK STARTED WHEN YOU SHOWED UP! ONE MORE PHONEY MOVE AN' I'LL CROAK YOU, S'HELP ME!

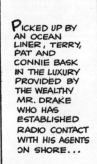

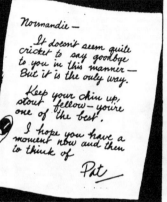

GEE, BEING STUCK IN THIS JAIL WAITIN' FOR THAT FORGERY CHARGE IS BAD ENOUGH, BUT HAVIN' NUTHIN' TO READ IS WORSE!

I HAVE AN IDEA!

WOULD YOU SEE IF YOU COULD DIG US UP SOMETHING TO READ?

YOU'RE NOT BAD BLOKES— I'LL SEE WOT I CAN DO FOR YOU!

'ERE'S A VOLUME I FOUND IN TH' HINSPECTOR'S OFFICE—I 'OPES IT'LL PASS TH' TIME!

THANKS!

SWELL! WHAT'S TH' TITLE?

"20,000 YEARS IN SING SING"!!!

MILTON CANIFF

I SUPPOSE WHEN THIS AGENT OF DRAKE'S GETS HERE TO ACCUSE US OF FORGERY WE'LL BE TAKEN TO UNITED STATES TERRITORY FOR TRIAL.. IF WE CAN'T PROVE OUR INNOCENCE WE MAY GET FROM ONE TO TWENTY YEARS IN THE PEN!

CONNIE, WHAT DO THEY DO TO FORGERS IN YOUR COUNTRY?

OH, IF CHINEE CHEATS RICH MERCHANT HE IS TAKEN OUT IN NIGHT AN' THUMPED ON NOODLE... THEN HE IS MAYBE HUNG UP BY TOES...

PLEHAPS, IF MERCHANT TOUGHISH GUY HE HAS CHEATER'S HANDS CUT OFF SO NO MORE CAN MAKE FALSE SCRIBBLES.... VELLY SIMPLE...

MILTON CANIFF

..MY COUNTRY 'TIS ♫ OF THEE.. ♫

?

'EY WHO WAS THAT HI 'EARD SINGIN' "GOD SAVE TH' KING"?

GWAN! WE WUZ SINGIN' "AMERICA"!

BLAWST YE! "HAMERICA", INDEED!— HIT'S A BLOOMIN' PARODY ON "GOD SAVE TH' KING"!— YE REBELS!

LOOK OUT, PAT!— OL' CORNWALLIS IS GONNA SIC TH' HESSIANS ON US!

LEMME SEE— HI COME IN 'ERE T' TELL YOU 'BLOKES SUMTHIN'!— NOW WOT WUZ IT?

MILTON CANIFF

HO!— HI GOT HIT!— MR DRAKE'S AGENT IS OUTSIDE WAITIN' TO 'ACCUSE YE!— NOW YE'LL CATCH HIT— OR HI AIN'T A FOOT 'IGH!

!!

!!

GEE, PAT! DRAKE'S AGENT IS HERE TO ACCUSE US OF FORGERY!— WHAT DO WE DO NOW?

FIRST WE'LL FIND OUT WHAT IT'S ALL ABOUT!

YES— BUT THEN WHAT?— GOLLY, WE'RE INNOCENT!— BUT HOW CAN WE HIRE LAWYERS TO COMPETE WITH DRAKE'S STAFF OF HIGH PRICED LEGAL BRAINS?

WORRY ABOUT THAT WHEN THE TIME COMES!— NOW LET'S GO IN AND FACE DRAKE'S AGENT!— AND HOPE HE'S ABLE TO LISTEN TO REASON!

?

GOOD GOLLY!

IT'S NORMANDIE!!!

YESSIR, BOYS! IT'S YOUR LITTLE RAY OF SUNSHINE!

MILTON CANIFF

USHERED INTO THE PRISON OFFICE TO MEET THEIR ACCUSER, TERRY PAT AND CONNIE ARE AMAZED TO FIND NORMANDIE DRAKE WAITING FOR THEM....

7-1

WELL, BOYS—YOU DON'T SEEM VERY HAPPY TO SEE ME—AND YOU REALLY SHOULD, YOU KNOW!

IF YOU'RE NOT TOO BUSY LAUGHING AT US—WOULD YOU MIND, EXPLAINING WHAT THIS IS ALL ABOUT?

OF COURSE ..WHEN I WASN'T ABLE TO FIND YOU IN SINGAPORE I REMEMBERED THE TEN THOUSAND DOLLAR CHECK MY UNCLE GAVE CONNIE...

..KNOWING,THAT TO CASH SUCH A LARGE CHECK YOU'D GO TO THE BANK IT WAS DRAWN ON, I RADIOED THEM TO HOLD YOU AS FORGERS. I SIGNED THE MESSAGE "DRAKE" WHICH IS, AFTER ALL, MY NAME!.. AND THAT, CHILDREN, IS HOW AUNTIE NORMANDIE CAUGHT UP WITH THE THREE LIL' RUNAWAY PIGGIES!

WANTED!

I SUPPOSE YOU THINK IT WAS PRETTY SMART TO HAVE THE SINGAPORE POLICE HOLD TERRY, CONNIE AND ME FOR FORGERY!

YES!—FRANKLY, I THINK IT WAS PRETTY DARNED SMART!

7-2

BUT I DON'T UNDERSTAND YOU, NORMANDIE!—WHY ARE YOU FOLLOWING US? WHY SHOULD A GIRL LIKE YOU WANT THE COMPANY OF THREE TRAMPS LIKE US?

THREE OF YOU?—ARE YOU BLIND?—I'M IN LOVE WITH YOU—NOT TERRY AND CONNIE!—AS FAR AS I'M CONCERNED THEY DON'T EXIST!

OH GULLYWUMPS! WE IS NUTHIN' BUT SPOOKS—JUS' HAUNTS IN TH' HOOSYGOW!

A PRETTY CHEAP TRICK, I CALL IT! YOU HAVE US HELD ON A FORGERY CHARGE—THEN YOU INSULT MY PALS!

I TAKE IT YOU'RE NONE TOO HAPPY TO SEE ME!

7-3

NO!

..AND WHAT'S MORE—I'M GOING TO SEE THAT YOU GET SHIPPED BACK TO YOUR UNCLE AT ONCE!

INDEED?

...YOU FORGET THAT YOU ARE STILL IN JAIL, PAT RYAN!—AND LITTLE NORMANDIE IS GOING TO LET ALL OF YOU LANGUISH HERE UNTIL YOU CHANGE YOUR TUNE!

HOLY SMOKE! NOW SHE'S GONNA DESERT US!

F' MERCY GOO'NESS—PLETTY MISSY LEAVE IN PLETTY MESSY! WOE!

YOU MEAN TO TELL ME YOU'D ALLOW TERRY AND CONNIE AND ME TO STAY IN THIS JAIL ON A FALSE FORGERY CHARGE JUST BECAUSE I WON'T JUMP WHEN YOU CRACK THE WHIP?

THAT'S ABOUT IT!

7-4

I MAY BE SPOILED—BUT WHEN I WANT SOMETHING I GET IT!—I'LL MAKE YOU FALL IN LOVE WITH ME IF I HAVE TO KEEP YOU AND YOUR PALS IN JAIL ALL SUMMER!

THAT'S A DARN FUNNY WAY TO GO ABOUT IT!

GOLLY—TH' FOURTH OF JULY!—AN HERE WE ARE IN THE HANDS OF TH' BRITISH—JUS' LIKE TH' COLONISTS IN 1776!

KINDA LIKE TH' FOURTH IN TH' UNITED STATES, THOUGH!—OL' PAT'S BEIN' INDEPENDENT—AN' NORMANDIE'S FURNISHIN' TH' FIREWORKS!

SINGAPORE

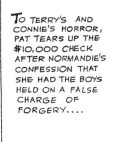